A Place
in the Sun

A Place in the Sun

by Jill Rubalcaba

Clarion Books ✳ New York

Clarion Books
a Houghton Mifflin Company imprint
215 Park Avenue South, New York, NY 10003

Text copyright © 1997 by Jill Rubalcaba

The text is set in 14/18-point Weiss.

For information about this and other Houghton Mifflin trade and reference
books and multimedia products, visit The Bookstore at Houghton Mifflin on
the World Wide Web at (http://www.hmco.com/trade/).

Library of Congress Cataloging-in-Publication Data

Rubalcaba, Jill.
A place in the sun / Jill Rubalcaba
p. cm
Summary: In ancient Egypt, the gifted young son of a sculptor is taken into
slavery when he attempts to save his father's life, and is himself almost killed
before his exceptional talent leads Pharaoh to name him Royal Sculptor.
ISBN 0-395-82645-4
1. Egypt—Civilization—To 332 B.C.—Juvenile Fiction.
[1. Egypt—Civilization—To 332 B.C.—Fiction. 2. Sculptors—Fiction.
3. Fathers and sons—Fiction.]   I. Title
PZ7.R8276P1 1997
[Fic]—dc20   96–38635
                                                                        CIP
                                                                        AC

BP   10   9   8   7   6   5   4   3   2   1

For my parents, who are my sun.
Love always,
Jill

CONTENTS

A Place in the Sun

Thirteenth Century B.C., Egypt

Hunger drove the cobra from the Land of the Ghosts into the man village. She slithered along a garden wall searching for food. Searching. She stopped to taste the night air for danger. Then slithered farther into the place where humans lived. Stopping now and then, cautious, and searching.

On the other side of the garden wall a mouse nibbled seed in the sand beside a grain silo. The cobra sensed the mouse's scratching. *Food.* She slipped into a crack in the mud-brick wall. The cobra couldn't see the mouse, but she could feel it. She flicked her tongue, tasting the dust. Flick. Dust tasting of mouse. Flick. *Food.*

The cobra rippled toward the grain silo. Rising up and spreading her hood, she swayed from side to side. Searching.

With deadly speed she struck. And struck again. The mouse, paralyzed by the poison, fell on its side, heaving its last breaths. There was no hurry now, but the cobra, starved for so long, wasted no time and swallowed it whole.

Now that the cobra's hunger was satisfied, she began to feel another discomfort. Cold. Sluggish from her meal, she looked for cover nearby. On the garden bench she found a toolbox and slid inside. She wrapped around the stone tools still warm from the day's sun and fell into a heavy sleep.

CHAPTER 1

The Festival of Opet

Senmut danced around his father, tugging on his linen kilt. "It's time to go. Hurry, Father."

"Time to go where?" Yuf tapped his jaw, pretending to think hard.

"The parade," Senmut said, frustrated by the delay. "Everyone will be at the river before we get there."

Last year the crowd had swelled in front of Senmut, blocking his view. He'd hopped up and down on his toes, but still he hadn't been able to see. The roads overflowed with people who had come to see the parade. Senmut had never heard so many strange languages.

Just as the Pharaoh turned the bend in the road, the crowd surged forward, pressing Senmut out. By the time he wormed his way to the front, Ramses II had passed, and all he could see was the backs of bald heads belonging to the priests.

He had run to the Nile, dodging donkey and foreigner, hoping to watch the priests load the golden statue of the god Amun onto the royal barge, but the crowd was too thick. He never made it to the river's edge. He had fallen into the dust. His tears had mingled with the dirt.

"I don't want to miss Amun again this year."

"Yuf, don't tease the boy," Senmut's mother, Nofret, scolded.

Yuf planted a loud kiss on Nofret's cheek. She swatted at him, ducking her head to hide her smile.

Yuf laughed. "I'll carry you on my shoulders. You'll see Amun this time. But first some breakfast."

Breakfast? Senmut wasn't the tiniest bit hungry. He could already hear the musicians in the village street. Who could think of food at a time like this?

He danced around his mother, who was cooking sweetmeats on the roof.

"Run down to the grain silo and fetch me some grain, Senmut. You can grind it to flour while we wait for breakfast to cook."

Senmut hopped down the steps, thrusting out one leg, then the other. A reed basket lay propped against his father's toolbox. Senmut swept it up and put it on his head. He danced around the bench to the music coming over the garden wall from the street outside.

The mice have been into the grain again, I see. Where is that lazy cat? Senmut called for the cat. "Minkah!"

Senmut thought he heard stirring from under the toolbox. He bent to look under the bench, expecting to find Minkah stretching out of a nap.

"Minkah, you worthless mouser!" But Senmut was surprised to see nothing but sand.

The music on the other side of the garden wall grew louder. The street musicians were just outside Senmut's house. Senmut scooped grain into the basket and ran up the stairs two at a time.

He poured some grain into the stone bowl by his mother and crushed it with a heavy stone pestle. But he was too excited to grind for long. He ran to the edge of the roof. There were acrobats in the street below.

"Look, a juggler. He has five clubs in the air. He's throwing them as high as our roof. If he came a bit closer, I could catch one." Senmut leaned way out, reaching with one hand. The juggler below laughed and spun the clubs closer and closer to Senmut.

"Don't lean out so far—you'll fall," Nofret warned.

"Such a worrier. Do you worry over me so?" Yuf puckered his lips like a fish. Nofret giggled and leaned back. She smacked him with the reed basket. "What, no kisses? Well then, come, Senmut. We can work a bit today."

Senmut couldn't believe what his father was saying. Work? Not today.

"Father, couldn't it wait? The Festival of Opet . . ."

"The festival lasts for weeks, and there is plenty of time before the parade begins." Yuf started down the stairs.

Senmut looked down at the streets. People laughed and danced. The musicians played. Senmut sighed. Well, his father would have to stop for breakfast. His mother would make sure of that. They might still leave early enough to get a good spot for the parade. But not early enough for Senmut. If he had his way, they would take their sweetmeats in a basket to eat at the river's edge.

After one last look and a wave to the jugglers, he followed his father down to the garden.

Next to the toolbox on the garden bench stood a small stone statue. A nobleman had commissioned Yuf to carve a likeness of the cat goddess Bastet. The nobleman planned to double his wheat planting this year and was taking all precautions. Bastet made the sun ripen the crops. It was wise to show respect.

Senmut picked up the statue and turned it from side to side. The cat looked straight ahead with quiet dignity. Bastet was sure to be pleased.

As excited as Senmut was about the parade, it slipped to the back of his mind once he took hold of the stone. Stone never failed to excite him—marble, granite, limestone . . . they all played their magic on Senmut, tingling with life in his hands. Reverently, Senmut positioned the statue on the workbench facing the heat of Re rising in the morning sky.

A block of alabaster had been delivered from far up the Nile the day before. A large piece. It was beautiful. Senmut ran his hands over the surface.

He had his father's gift, to see the spirit that dwelled within stone. At first he hadn't realized it was a gift. He thought surely everyone could see. The spirit was right there. How could they *not* see? But as he grew older and saw his friends back away from him, frightened, when he mentioned the stone spirits, he learned to keep quiet about them. His father told him that because the others could not see the image, they feared it. They thought it was an evil spirit, lurking in the shadows beyond their vision.

Yuf watched his son study the new stone. "One day soon you will have such a piece."

Senmut wished he could have *this* piece. He

did not want to wait for "one day." Wait for the parade, wait for his own stone, wait, wait, wait. Senmut was sick of waiting. He plopped down on the garden bench, took up the polishing cloth and the statue of Bastet, and started rubbing fiercely.

His father smiled at him.

Yuf reached into his toolbox for a chisel. He pulled his hand out quickly, grasping his wrist.

"Father, are you hurt?" Senmut was surprised. He saw the pain contort his father's face.

"Run," his father grunted through clamped teeth.

Senmut stood still, confused. Why did his father want him to run? From what? Then from the corner of his eye, Senmut saw the cobra waving in and out of his field of vision. He dared not move his head. The cobra had turned to him, swaying, searching for a deadly point of attack.

Yuf threw himself on the snake. "Run!" The cobra turned on Yuf like twists in lightning, striking over and over at his face and neck.

Looking frantically for something to hit the

snake with, Senmut felt the weight of the statue still in his hand. When the cobra reared to strike, he threw the statue at the cobra. It hit her square in the head, knocking her backward against the garden wall. The snake disappeared into a crack in the wall.

Senmut lunged for his father.

Yuf lay on the floor of the courtyard, his legs twisted under him awkwardly. Senmut pressed his ear to his father's heart. He heard nothing.

"Father!" Senmut shouted. Yuf's eyelids fluttered, then fell still again.

"Father." This time there was no response.

Nofret came to the top of the stairs.

"I can't hear his heart."

Nofret flew down the stairs. She grabbed Yuf's shoulders, pulling him to her, sobbing his name.

Senmut rushed for the gate, shouting, "I'll get the physician." He clawed at the latch, yanked open the heavy door, and ran into the street.

He stood in the street, disoriented. The music, the crowds—he'd forgotten the festival. He grabbed a boy skipping by. "Quickly, run for the physician. My father—he's dying—the cobra's poison." Senmut's own words choked him.

Kaswan, the village elder, broke through the wild crowd, pushing aside those who blocked his way.

"Come." Kaswan grabbed Senmut's elbow, steering him back to his father.

The music in the streets still rose and fell, but inside the courtyard it sounded distant, muffled by the murmurs of the neighbors who had crowded the gate.

Those who followed only out of curiosity glanced about uneasily, searching the corners and shadows for evil spirits. But those who knew Yuf or knew of his art mumbled prayers for the well-being of his ka. Their prayers for his father's spirit only made Senmut more anxious. Could his ka be preparing the way to the other world?

Kaswan, Senmut, and Nofret knelt around Yuf, looking for signs of life. His breast rose and fell so slightly, Senmut couldn't tell if it was really moving at all.

The physician hurried into the courtyard. He was out of breath from the run. He clutched to his heaving chest a medical bag woven of papyrus reed and a scroll of treatments. The crowd parted to make way for him.

"O ghost, thou hidden one, concealer, trickster, dwelling in this man's flesh, get thee hence! Escape!" The physician's voice grew louder. "O demon, destroyer of organs, I order thee to leave this man."

The physician knelt to examine Yuf. He felt for a pulse. "His heart is weak and irregular." He looked around. "You and you and you," he said, pointing to the strongest in the crowd, "lift him gently."

The men carefully placed Yuf on his sleeping mat under the canopy on the roof, cradling his head in the headrest.

The physician unpacked his medical bag. He lined up packets of dried herbs, magic charms, and vials of liquids in neat rows along-side Yuf. Yuf groaned.

The physician raised a curved bone knife with one hand; his other hand cupped over Yuf's brow. He squeezed his eyes shut and prayed. Only his lips moved.

At first Senmut thought the physician meant to cut Yuf with the knife. He'd heard of physicians who believed in bleeding the evil spirits out.

Senmut searched the physician's face. Was there hope? Would his father die? The old man's expression gave away nothing.

Senmut grabbed his father's hand. He held tight. He was afraid to let go. Afraid if he did, Yuf's ka would drain away into the Egyptian sand. Senmut held tighter, leaned closer. His lips began to move in a prayer of his own.

The physician scored the plaster around Yuf's sleeping mat with the knife carved with the Eye of Horus. Then he looked up and spoke to Senmut for the first time. "A barrier to protect him from evil spirits."

Senmut looked at the small channel etched by the knife. How could such a scratch protect

Yuf from evil? "He'll be all right, won't he? You can make it so, can't you?"

He felt his mother tug at him. Too late he realized what he'd done. What if the physician declared Yuf untreatable? Yuf would die without the physician's help—without spells, amulets, ointments. Why had he asked? Why was he always so impatient? His father needed the physician's skill. He mustn't hurry the old man.

The physician gently lifted Yuf's head and slid the U-shaped headrest out from under Yuf's neck, replacing it with one from his reed medicine bag. The base of the pedestal was carved, a serpent armed with a knife. Senmut closed his eyes and saw the cobra striking Yuf. Striking again and again. What would become of his father?

The physician said, "His heart speaks out; the voice falters. We shall have to wait and see if it grows strong . . . or stumbles."

The physician lifted the stopper from a large vessel. He poured the potion into a small cup he held at arm's length. He turned his head and leaned back as he poured.

What was that smell? Senmut wrinkled his nose. It smelled like rotting flesh and decaying plants.

"To drive the evil spirits from his body." The physician pressed the cup to Yuf's lips. Senmut retched. He held his stomach, squeezing, trying to control the spasms.

The physician warned, "Beware the fire beneath the flesh. The reddened skin is like the red sands of the desert. It brings death."

Senmut looked at his father. Yuf's chest shuddered. He struggled for each breath. Was this his father? His loud, joking father? Lying here scarcely able to breathe? It couldn't be. Senmut wanted him to wake up. To open his eyes and wink at Senmut as though it were all some joke. *It's not funny, Father. This is not funny.*

CHAPTER 3
The Spirit of the Healer

"How is he?" Kaswan asked Nofret, stepping out of the shadows.

"The physician is casting spells." Nofret looked dazed.

Kaswan nodded. "I sent the others away."

Senmut turned away from them and paced the courtyard in long, angry strides. He felt helpless against the cobra's poison. *There has to be something,* he thought. *I can't just let him die. The gods would not have made a gift of the alabaster if they wanted him to die.*

Senmut stood in front of the alabaster, his legs spread wide, his fists pressed into his waist. *Father can't die. He just can't.*

A new thought pierced Senmut. It prickled him with shame. *I wanted this stone. This stone belonging to Father. I wanted it. I wished for it. I betrayed Father with my own selfishness.*

Senmut pressed his cheek against the cold, hard rock. *I didn't want it like this. Not this way. The gods must know, not like this.*

At first Senmut thought it was his own breath he heard. He held it and listened. And then he heard the whispers. From within the stone.

Had it spoken? Yes. The spirit trapped inside the stone. The spirit Sekhmet. The spirit of the healer.

Could he release her? Until now he had carved only small sections of his father's work, learning how each tool marked the stone, learning with how much force he must swing the mallet. Sometimes his father would give him a flawed stone for practice, but always Senmet's impatience, his chisel driven too deep, ruined the stone.

This was not practice. His father's life was in the balance. Delight Sekhmet with her image, and she might choose to use her powers to cure Father. Anger Sekhmet, and . . . Senmut did not want to think what might happen then. He flattened his palms against his ears, but still the whispers came.

Kaswan pulled Senmut's hands from his ears. "You must listen to the spirit voices."

"Can you hear them too?" Senmut asked.

Kaswan smiled. "I can see that you hear them, as your father heard."

"How do I know what to do?"

"You must listen to your inner voice."

"But what if I do the wrong thing?"

Senmut remembered a time Yuf had stayed mad at him for days. Senmut had been in a hurry. Like always. But it was a day fit for the gods, and his friends were going fishing. Senmut was to deliver a small statue his father had carved. He was to meet his friends at the river. He was in a hurry. He ran.

When he fell in the marketplace, the statue slipped from his hands and shattered. A month of his father's hard work gone, because of his impatience. His father had punished him. Made him sit and watch the lotus blossom open and close. To teach him patience, Yuf had said.

Senmut whispered to Kaswan, "I am afraid I will make a mistake."

"Your inner voice will guide you."

Senmut thought of what his inner voice had told him the day he had broken the statue. He had convinced himself such a fine day should not be wasted on an errand. He'd argued with his inner voice until it was silent.

Kaswan put a hand on Senmut's shoulder. "The inner voice is in concert with the honorable deed, in conflict with the dishonorable one. You will know."

The spirit voice from within the stone called out to Senmut. He tried to listen to his inner voice. But he was afraid. Afraid if he failed, it would mean his father's death.

Kaswan handed Senmut the chisel.

Senmut turned it in his hand. The fear began to disappear. He forgot the broken statue, forgot Kaswan, forgot even his father, lying near death on the roof above him. He could see into the stone. He could see the carving. Senmut placed the chisel on the stone and raised the mallet.

The clang of stone on stone rang in the courtyard.

❋

Senmut carved the alabaster block for two days without rest. When darkness fell, Senmut lit torches and continued to chisel. Lighting an oil lamp, Senmut thought, *The sun god, Re, drives his chariot into battle with chaos. I must fight my own demons here. If Re rises to light the morning sky, he has won. If my father rises, I have.*

Already the lion head of Sekhmet was emerging from the stone.

Nofret dragged down the stairs, a washbasin sloshing at her hip. Her shoulders sagged. Her eyes, rimmed in red, were underlined with dark crescents. She had not slept in the two days since Yuf had lost consciousness. Senmut did not ask about his father. He hadn't asked the last few times she'd come down. There was no need. He could see in her face that there was no change.

She dumped the cloudy water in the dirt

beside the well, not even bothering to wet the earth beneath the fig tree. She filled the basin with clear, fresh water.

Kaswan dozed in the shade, propped up against the column. Senmut let him sleep. Someone should sleep. He was glad Kaswan had stayed. The wise one's presence spoke of Yuf's importance to the spirits.

Senmut turned back to his work. He was tired. The strength he had started with was seeping away, and in its place were aches in his shoulders from raising the heavy tools.

His father had always been there for guidance, direction. In his weariness Senmut began to worry that he had been wrong to take the stone. Who was he to try to please a god? He was just a boy. The waters of the Nile had overflowed but nine times since his birthing day. How could he have thought himself worthy?

Senmut's arms hung by his sides.

Behind him he heard Nofret's sharp intake of breath. Senmut turned to see what had startled her. She was staring at the stone. Her hand flew to her lips.

Kaswan stood behind her, smiling. He took her by the elbow to steady her. "Your son has been touched by the gods."

Senmut turned back to his carving. The lion's mane flowed over the rock like water. The ripples melted into one another, changing the alabaster to fluid, flowing in the sunlight. It was good. He was good. Kaswan thought so. His mother thought so.

Senmut picked up the chisel. He attacked the stone with new energy. More confident than before. If only he could finish before it was too late. He must hurry. Hurry.

A dove fluttered down to the top of the courtyard wall. The clanging of the chisel and Senmut's swinging arm made the bird nervous, but the seeds in the dirt were tempting. The dove glided to the top of the cone-shaped grain silo. She cocked her head from side to side, twisting and pivoting to keep one eye on the seeds in the dirt below.

A clang of the chisel drove her back to the courtyard wall; then in one courageous swoop she fell on the seeds. Pecking at them, she grew less cautious, absorbed with eating the meats from the shells she cracked with her beak.

Senmut needed the small chisel for some fine work around Sekhmet's nose. Hastily, he tossed the large chisel to the side. It struck the dove. She lay beneath the discarded chisel, her neck broken.

Kaswan moaned.

Senmut turned, alarmed. Was his father worse?

Kaswan's face had gone ashen. He stared, pointing at the ground.

Senmut followed the direction of Kaswan's outstretched finger, fear flooding him. He saw the lifeless dove and for a moment stood uncomprehending. What was his chisel doing there, he wondered. And then he knew. All feeling left his body as if he had opened a vein into the sand. He wondered if he would fall, if his legs would hold him.

Kaswan whispered, "You know the penalty for killing a dove?"

Senmut knew. It was death.

CHAPTER 4
The Royal House

The Keeper of the Cloth rushed forward, the sheer robe draped over his arms billowing like sails luffing on the Nile.

The harpist closed her eyes against the racing crisscross of servants, but she couldn't close her ears to the slapping of their sandals echoing inside the royal chamber. She struggled to keep her tempo slow and soothing.

Ramses II sat, his head tilted back, while a Nubian slave outlined his eyes in black.

A servant bowed to the chief administrator and handed him a papyrus scroll. Neferronpet broke the seal.

The harpist in the corner ended her piece

and looked to Neferronpet for instructions. He nodded for her to continue. Her strokes tumbled, note over note, like water rippling over stones.

"No hunting today." Ramses fidgeted under the full-length linen tunic his slaves had pulled over his head. He preferred the freedom of the short kilt. The arthritis in his hip was bothering him again today.

"I'm afraid not, sir."

"Are the priests of Karnak ready?"

"They await your presence."

"Good. And all is ready at the temple of Luxor to receive the procession?"

"Messengers indicate that all is ready."

The Pharaoh's son Merneptah sat cross-legged in the corner on the limestone floor.

A servant darted across the chamber. She dropped to the ground at Ramses' feet, pressing her forehead to the floor. She held out an inlaid box, its lid thrown back.

Merneptah pretended the servant was presenting the jewels to him. *I am the Pharaoh,* he thought, *the Divine One. The harp is plucked for my pleasure. My subjects line the streets, waiting for days*

*for just a glimpse of me. I raise my hand and women
faint and grown men cry. They tell their grandchildren
the story of the day I passed inches from them.*

A servant rushed past Merneptah. The
breeze in the wake of her skirts roused him
from his daydream.

"Father, will I be allowed inside the temple?"
Merneptah asked. He wanted to see the inner
sanctum. Once, escaping the watchful eye of
his nurse, he had woven his way among the
columns to the great hall. But he had stopped
there. He was frightened. What secrets were
inside? Only the priests and his father were
allowed to enter. He was afraid the gods
would curse him if he looked into the sacred
chamber. He had let his nurse find him far
from the temple of Karnak, so no one would
see his fear and remember it.

Ramses smiled at his son. He knew that
Merneptah dreamed of being Pharaoh, just as
he had when his father, Seti, had ruled. "You
will wait with your brothers and sisters until
the procession begins. Then you will follow
me just as Amun's son follows him."

The Keeper of the Diadem entered the

room, bowed his head, and presented the solar headdress. Four golden cobras coiled the ram's head, wrapping around the horns, each balancing a solar disk on its hood. In the center of the crown a fifth cobra stood, symbol of the divine rule.

"Will there be crowds?" Merneptah asked, unrolling his sitting mat by his father's feet. His slave rushed in to help, but Merneptah brushed him aside.

Ramses raised one eyebrow at Neferronpet, who smiled behind the scroll and raised the unfurled papyrus higher to hide his amusement. Merneptah would one day see that there was more to being Pharaoh than being cheered by crowds. Neferronpet chuckled, then cleared his throat and faked a cough to disguise the sound.

"All in the Two Lands will cheer you, my son." Ramses bent over to allow the keeper to place the headdress on his head.

Ramses saw the broken seal on the scroll Neferronpet held. "What news of Abu Simbel?" Ramses asked his administrator.

"The engineers are surveying the site."

"Only freshly cut stones. At Abu Simbel I'll have no defacing of the tombs of those who came before me."

"They believe the temple can be cut into the cliffs. No additional stone should be necessary."

Ramses raised an eyebrow, waiting for more. It was not like his administrator to give short answers. "What is it, Neferronpet?"

"It's nothing, really, just rumor from the guard. They were sent to arrest a boy this morning, no older than Merneptah."

"What caused you to think of this?"

"The cobras, your Majesty." Neferronpet pointed to the headdress. "This boy's father was bitten by a cobra."

"What crime is that?"

"I would not have heard of it if it weren't for the statue."

"Statue?"

"It seems the boy was carving a statue of Sekhmet. He hoped to please her, that she might rid his father of the cobra's poison." Neferronpet carefully rolled the papyrus scroll closed. "The guards speak of it in whispers.

When they arrested the boy, they swear the statue cursed them."

"A boy carved this statue that causes my guards to tremble? I still see no reason to arrest him. My trembling guards, though . . ."

"He killed a dove, Great One."

"Perhaps the statue itself is cursed."

A servant adjusted an embroidered belt around the Pharaoh's waist.

"The guards seem to think not, Beloved of Amun. They seem to feel the statue intends to protect its creator from the executioner."

Merneptah tugged on the ankh that hung from his father's belt. "Couldn't this boy plead his case to Amun at the temple gates?"

The Pharaoh pulled the symbol of life from his son's hand. "You have been studying affairs of state." He was pleased. Something more than the crowds and the parades interested his son after all.

Eager to show his father how much he had learned, Merneptah raced on. "During the Festival of Opet anyone can appeal to the god's mercy. It is the way. The courts would surely find him guilty, but with Amun there is always a chance for mercy."

Ramses put a hand on the boy's flushed cheek. "It shall be done." To Neferronpet he said, "Send a messenger."

Merneptah knew he had pleased his father. *Someday I will make him really proud, he will smile from his tomb in the west,* he thought. *When I am Pharaoh the people will worship me like no other. I will stand in the temple hall and they will chant my name. Merneptah, Merneptah, Merneptah . . .*

"Merneptah." His mother's voice blended with the chant, then broke into his daydream. "You are not bathed yet, Merneptah. Hurry. It is nearly time for the procession."

CHAPTER 5
Trial at Karnak

The forest of stone columns rose all around Senmut, towering out of sight. He felt small. Even Kaswan, walking next to him, slowed when they entered the great hall.

Shaven priests, draped in white linen, stood at the base of each column waving pots of incense to purify the air.

Senmut thought he should feel scared or worried or even sick. He should feel something. But he found himself wondering how the hairless priests removed their eyelashes. Odd, he thought, to be thinking of eyelashes now, when soon he could be dead.

A guard grabbed Kaswan. "You must get in line with the others, old man."

"We have come to plead our case before the great and just god Amun." Kaswan jerked his arm from the guard's grip.

"Then enter by the chamber of Thoth." The guard pointed to a doorway.

Kaswan grabbed Senmut's elbow and pushed past the guard.

Inside, holy men fanned the air with giant ostrich feathers. Senmut felt the skin on the back of his neck prickle. The golden statue of Amun seemed to breathe, its heart to beat. With arms folded across his chest, Amun looked down at Senmut. The god could look kind or stern, loving or vengeful, calm or angry. He held all emotion. Senmut knew his thoughts were a sacrilege, but he couldn't stop them. What of the sculptor who had created this living metal? What of the mere mortal who had molded a lump of gold into a living god? What marvels he could learn from such a man!

A river of peasants flowed through the great

hall to see Amun, the king of all gods. Many
had waited hours in the heat for this moment.
The royal guard herded them, prodding anyone who stopped. The guards were kept busy,
for many paused. Senmut watched them. One
peasant looked scared, another smiled, many
cried. Each saw something different in the face
of Amun.

Kaswan fell to the floor at Amun's feet.
He grabbed Senmut's wrist and yanked him
to the ground. Then with outstretched
hands, Kaswan held the sacred scroll of
laws. "O Spirit-That-Moves-All-Living-Things,
hear your humble servant in defense of
Senmut, who still bears the sidelock of youth."

A priest stepped forward and signaled
Kaswan to rise but ignored Senmut, flattened
to the ground in penance.

"Senmut did not mean to bring the bird
from the heavens," Kaswan said. "He was
sculpting the image of Sekhmet, hoping to
persuade her to use her healing power to drive
a plague from his household. It was not the
sacred Ibis or the holy Hawk but merely a
dove. We seek your mercy, O-Hidden-One."

The anguish in Kaswan's voice could be heard in the chamber long after his words were still. Several peasants turned to Kaswan, curious, but the guards pushed them along.

Senmut pressed himself to the stone floor. He listened to the papyrus sandals scratching the stone as the hordes of peasants passed. They whispered, like judges discussing his fate.

Then the whispering stopped. The whole line came to a standstill. Even the guards paused in their duties to watch the great Amun. All waited for his judgment. Would the boy be pierced through by a spike and hang on the banks of the Nile? Or would Amun show mercy?

Amun bent forward. The movement was so slight that later the peasants argued whether or not the statue had moved at all.

A priest came from behind the statue and approached Kaswan, his hands hidden in the folds of his linen tunic. "It is the mercy of Amun that spares the life of the boy. It is Amun's wish that he serve his remaining suns in the gold mines of Nubia."

No one moved. Even the fan bearers paused.

The silence was like being buried in sand. Nubia. Death was more merciful. Only the worst criminals worked the mines. To work the gold mines meant to exist with the sting of the foreman's whip licking your back, the flies living off your wounds. Death came slowly, torturously, step by step, from starvation and thirst.

Two of the royal guards came forward and picked Senmut up by his forearms. Senmut hung limp between the guards. They hauled him from the Temple and through the streets. Senmut hung his head, watching his feet drag along the packed sand, surprised when they bled because he felt nothing. The guards up ahead shoved the peasants out of the way.

The streets were overflowing. The parade had begun. Musicians banging tambourines led the way, dancers followed in a swirl of sheer fabric. The guards pulled Senmut against the flow of the parade in the street. Senmut was so close, he could have reached out and touched the paraders. He would never get closer. But Senmut saw nothing. Nothing but the blood of his feet trailing in the sand.

CHAPTER 6
The Desert

Senmut felt as though stones were tied to his ankles. He dragged his feet along, stumbling over ridges in the sand. He was afraid if he fell, he wouldn't be able to get up again.

The heat made it difficult to breathe. The scorch of the desert bore down on him from above and reflected up from below, surrounding him in heat. Senmut pushed through the heat in slow motion, as if he were walking underwater. Water. How long had it been? His throat ached.

The man behind Senmut chanted his death song. Senmut plodded along to the man's words.

"O Breaker-of-Bones, I have not lied.

"O Eater-of-Entrails, I have not added to the weight of the balance.

"O Embracer-of-Fire, I have not built a dam against running water."

When they had started out across the desert, there had been fifty of them. Senmut was too weak to count, but he guessed they had lost at least ten so far. The first to drop was an old man. The guards whipped him until they tired, then left him where he lay. Not long after, Senmut heard the jackals howl. He looked back. In the distance, through the shimmering waves of heat, Senmut saw the squirming mass of wild dogs. He was glad he was too far to see more than a blob of brown fur, but even that much haunted him. That night Senmut dreamed of jackals snarling and tearing at his flesh. He awoke shivering from the night cold. Since then others had fallen. He hadn't looked back again.

Senmut watched a guard drink long from his water pouch. Senmut ran his swollen tongue over his cracked lips. He picked up a pebble to suck on, but it just stuck in his withered mouth.

"Make camp," the lead guard hollered back to the guards flanking the line of ragged prisoners.

Senmut fell to his knees. He waited for the guards to set out the water rations.

"Psst." Senmut felt a tap on his sunburned shoulder. He turned. It was the boy about his own age he'd noticed on the first day. By the end of that first march Senmut had stopped noticing anything but his own thirst and hunger. The boy was tattered and dusty, but he didn't look half dead like the rest of them.

"Look." Senmut followed the boy's finger to a line of ants marching down into a hole.

"So?" Senmut watched the guards. He had missed his ration of water the first day. He was careful not to let it happen again.

When the guard's back was turned, the boy dug in the sand. He pulled his fist from inside the anthill and then held out an open palm to Senmut. Senmut expected to see a handful of sand, but instead the boy's palm overflowed with seed. He poured it into Senmut's hand and pulled out another fistful. Senmut greedily ate the seed, licking his palm to get all of it.

The guard waved to Senmut to come get his

cup of water. Senmut wobbled to his feet. He had to force himself not to gulp it down. He rolled the water around in his mouth, back and forth across his tongue, before swallowing. The water was tepid and tasted of the mud bottom of the Nile, but it was wet and it was gone before his thirst was satisfied.

Senmut studied the other prisoners. He hadn't really looked at them since that first day. Their skin was blistered and peeling, hanging from their shrunken bones. The boy looked worn, too, but there was something different about him. Something unlike the others. His clothes were weatherworn, like theirs, and he was sunburned. What was different? His eyes. He watched everyone, everything. The rest sat dully staring into the space right in front of them. Senmut knew he too had sat just like that for days now. The boy sat quietly like the others, but he missed nothing. He was watching Senmut now.

Senmut returned his cup to the serving table and walked over to the boy.

"My name is Senmut. I am son of Yuf, master sculptor."

"I am Menkh, only son of Issa, Keeper of Royal Cattle."

"Why is it, Menkh, that the gods sent you here?"

"I fell asleep while tending my herd, and a stray damaged the dike at Luxor." Menkh looked Senmut straight in the eye, daring him to show disgust, but Senmut just nodded.

Senmut waited for Menkh to ask about his crime, but Menkh sat in silence.

"How is it you are not suffering like the rest of us?"

Menkh shrugged. "I have traveled through the desert before, with the cattle. There are tricks."

A black beetle scuttled across the sand by Menkh's feet. He snatched the scarab and popped it into his mouth. "They are crunchy, and not so tasty, but . . ."

Senmut had seen hundreds of scarabs scurry out of the way of his feet. A month ago the idea of eating an insect would have choked him, but now he'd eat anything to curb the pain that tortured his stomach. Maybe he could gain back some of his strength, he thought. Maybe he would survive the trip to Nubia. But then . . . he'd worry about that when they got there. If he could learn from Menkh to survive in the desert, perhaps there would be someone to teach him to survive the mines.

"Tomorrow we pass Tharu," Menkh said.

"I thought that place was just legend."

"I have been there."

"Is it true, then? The villagers have no noses?"

"Many criminals who have had their noses cut off move there. At least they can live in peace, without the stares. They can begin again."

"Will there be sand dwellers?" Senmut looked about him. He had heard tales of the bandits who would strip a caravan, not even leaving water. To take a desert traveler's water was an unforgivable crime. In the mines those guilty of it were found beaten to death by the other prisoners.

"There are always sand dwellers." Menkh shrugged. He didn't seem afraid of anything.

Senmut swallowed. "I can't sleep at night for

fear of the jackals. They haunt my dreams."

"You must learn the roar."

"The roar?"

Menkh tossed back his head and roared like a lion. It startled Senmut, it sounded so real. A few of the prisoners cried out, frightened of yet another danger. The guards laughed.

"That's amazing. I'd have sworn it was a real lion if I weren't sitting right next to you."

Menkh shrugged. "It moves a stubborn cow . . . and scares the jackals away . . . for a while, anyway."

Senmut tried to roar. This time the prisoners laughed too.

"No, like this. Feel my throat."

Menkh roared again. Senmut felt Menkh's throat—it vibrated. He tried it again.

"Much better, but deeper from here." Menkh pushed between Senmut's ribs.

By sunset Senmut sounded almost like a lion. He was not as good as Menkh, but maybe good enough to fool the jackals.

Shadows crept across the Red Land as the huge white ball that was Re sank into orange haze. The wind echoed through the dunes, shifting sand in clouds of dust. Copying Menkh, Senmut burrowed into the sand. The warm weight felt good on his tired muscles. *Tomorrow*, he thought, *I begin to survive.*

CHAPTER 7
The Mines of Nubia

The cook slopped a ladle of rations onto Senmut's plate. Senmut moved along the line, comparing water jugs to see which had the most. He tried not to look at his food. Although he had eaten insects in the desert, lots of them, he couldn't get used to seeing them surface and submerge in his dinner. But not eating meant death. And Senmut was not ready to die. Not yet.

He brought his dinner to where Menkh sat on a bench, apart from the others. "Gallery duty?"

Menkh was covered with soot. The overseers forced the small ones into the galleries, squeezing them through tunnels clawed out by the older men. If they came back, the air was safe to breathe. Many never returned. Menkh was small.

"Today, in the dark, I tripped."

Senmut waited. Menkh was shaken. In the weeks since they had become friends, it was the first time Senmut had seen him scared.

"I tripped over a body. I thought—I thought the air had killed him. I held my breath. But how long can you hold your breath? I was sure I would die, like the boy at my feet. Alone. In the dark."

"You are here."

"Yes, but how much longer?"

Senmut wanted to say something to give Menkh hope. But there was no hope. They would die here. Today, tomorrow, a year from now. They both knew it.

"I am going to escape."

"To where?" Senmut looked out over the endless sands. "The guards don't even bother watching us. They know no one can survive out there without water."

"I would rather die in the desert than in the dark by some poison in the air I can't see." Menkh grabbed Senmut's wrist. "Come with me."

"I can't."

"The statue?"

"I must finish it first. I don't know if my father lives or not. But I must do what I can."

"How much longer?"

Senmut thought. How much longer? Without tools, he had used what he could fashion from strips of cloth and stone. He'd even used his fingernails until they were worn to stubs. The wood he'd found in the mine, left behind by a torch carrier, was nearly carved. The lion's head of Sekhmet had come easily, the flow of the gnarled acacia lending itself to the lion's mane. But Sekhmet's graceful woman's body had taken time.

The most dangerous part was yet to come. He wanted to gild her. He'd found just the right stone for pounding gold into thin sheets. But he would have to smuggle gold past the scribes who weighed and recorded every nugget the prisoners brought out of the shafts. The scribes searched the prisoners thoroughly, even checking their ears.

But Zuka had found a way. Senmut had seen him palming flecks and nuggets to bribe the cook for extra rations and the guards for special treatment. Zuka had found a way to get the gold past the scribes. Senmut had been watching. He hadn't discovered Zuka's method. Not yet. But he would. He would wait and watch. There would be gold for Sekhmet.

"How long?" Menkh asked again.

Senmut shook his head. "I don't know." *Menkh is impatient,* Senmut thought. *Not so long ago I was just like him. When did I change?*

"I can't wait."

Senmut nodded. Menkh had made up his mind. Senmut knew he would have died on the journey if it hadn't been for Menkh's knowledge of the desert. He owed his life to Menkh. Senmut would miss his only friend. "May Isis protect you."

"Thank you, my friend."

They both sat quietly, knowing this would be their last time together.

❀

With Menkh gone, Senmut spent every moment watching Zuka. Zuka put no effort into his work, but the guards never whipped him to move faster or cut his rations for producing less than the others. While the prisoners wasted and died, one by one, Zuka remained soft and fat.

The prisoners slept soundly. The day's work left them dreamless. Zuka was not careful leaving the camp at night. What did he have to fear? He paid the guards well. The prisoners snored loudly. Senmut rose to follow, careful not to let Zuka see him. He needn't have worried. Zuka walked straight to the burial chamber without turning once.

The dead were carted from the shafts and thrown into a heap in a chamber near the mines. The pile grew, and when no more bodies could be stacked, the tomb was sealed and another dug.

Senmut slipped into the burial room behind Zuka. He hid among the rocks by the entrance. Zuka picked through the bodies, searching the day's dead, rolling aside the others.

Senmut wanted to run. He looked into the shadows for Anubis, guardian of the dead. Surely Anubis would strike Zuka dead for this dishonor to those journeying to the afterlife. It was unthinkable. Who was this Zuka? Senmut shuddered.

Zuka crammed his hand into the mouth of a young boy. Senmut almost cried out. Zuka pulled out a golden nugget. So this was how Zuka did it. He didn't smuggle the gold out himself—he hid it in the bodies of the dead.

Zuka ripped a square of cloth from the shredded garment of an old man. He wrapped the nugget in the cloth, tucked it in his waistband, then continued searching, prodding the pile with one foot.

Senmut knew that even for the life of his father he could not do this to the dead. All those weeks of watching Zuka had been for nothing. Senmut thought of Menkh and wished he were with his friend. What was the point of living now? It would be better to die in the desert alongside his friend than alone here, to have his body thrown on the heap, or worse, fed to the jackals.

Zuka finished collecting the nuggets and sat down on top of the pile of bodies to examine his gold. He held each nugget up, turning it in the dim light, weighing it in the palm of his hand.

Senmut was trapped behind the rocks. He couldn't leave without being seen until Zuka left. He felt sick, watching Zuka's treatment of the dead. When would the grave robber return to camp? Senmut was weary. He worked the backbreaking tunnels all day and carved each night when the others had fallen asleep. The promise of the statue had kept him alive. Until now. He felt tired. He wanted to lie in the pile of the dead and sleep forever.

Finally Zuka rose to leave. He picked a small nugget from his cloth and placed it on top of the rock by the entrance. A bribe for the guard?

Senmut held his breath. He waited until he was sure Zuka had disappeared into the night. Then he snatched the nugget and melted into the darkness.

Senmut sneaked back to camp, circling the mines. He was near the edge of the camp when he heard something. It sounded like a wounded animal. Senmut stayed perfectly still. The jackal? Had Anubis come? Again the low wail, longer this time. The jackal. Senmut raised his head and roared. The night turned so still, Senmut could hear his own heartbeat. He thought of Menkh somewhere out there. Was he still alive? It wasn't possible. Not without water.

Senmut hurried back to camp. He knew time was running out. He must finish the statue before it was too late.

❋

Senmut lay among the plague ridden. The guards never checked carefully here. They walked quickly by, covering their noses when they passed. Even the other prisoners slept as far from the sick as they could. Senmut had buried his nugget alongside his carving under his sleeping mat. He had wanted to begin pounding the gold right away, but he knew he needed his rest if he was to survive long enough to finish.

❁

Each night he worked a little later, getting less rest from the hardships of the day but driven by the fear he'd be too late to save his father.

The sheet of gold, hammered thin, was perfect. Senmut had pounded the nugget with painstaking slowness, the groans of the sick and the wounded veiling the dull thud of his rock on the gold.

Now he wrapped the statue in the gold sheet, pressing the thin metal into the crevices of the carving. Sekhmet came alive in his hands. His work was done.

Senmut was so pleased with his amulet, so relieved to be finally finished, he failed to hear the prisoner creep up behind him.

"You'll get us all whipped to death."

Senmut hid the statue behind him, but too late. "Mind your own business, old man." The man looked old and haggard, but that meant nothing here. He could be near Senmut's age. The mines aged them all.

"Keeping alive *is* my business. Some fool steals gold and we'll all be killed as an example to the others."

"What does it matter? We're going to die here one way or another."

"Maybe for you." The old man started yelling. "Guard, guard!"

Senmut had no place to run.

CHAPTER 8
The Plague

A plague struck Thebes. Thousands died. At first there was hope the great house would escape the ravages of the disease, but it crept inside the palace walls. Merneptah lay soaked in sweat. His body ached. One moment he was burning with fever; the next he shook so hard, Ramses threw his body across his son's to give him warmth and keep him from falling to the floor.

The room overflowed with physicians. Some chanted, others prepared medicines. So many were pounding their pestles, the chamber sounded more like a construction site than a sickroom.

Merneptah pressed his temples with his fingertips. "Father, make them stop the pounding. My head hurts."

Ramses raged, "You fools, take your thumping outside." He flung a bowl into the corridor, kicking the physician out behind it. "Can no one find me a physician who knows his business? I don't care if you must travel to the Land of Punt—find me a man who can cure my son."

Neferronpet ordered runners to search the kingdom for yet another physician. He wondered if there were any left. "It is time for the offering, my lord."

Ramses was reluctant to leave his son's bedside, but it would not be wise to anger the gods now. He pulled the ankh that hung around his neck over his head and rested the life sign on his son's heart. "I must wear the leopard skin now, my son. I'll be back as soon as I can."

"Pray for me, Father."

"I do nothing but."

Nefertari entered the room. The physicians

stopped chanting mid word. Ramses' first wife
was as beautiful as the stories told. She gently
stroked her husband's cheek. "You must eat
and get some rest—even the Great One must.
I will sit with Merneptah." Nefertari was worried about Ramses' health. All day and night
he sat with his son from his second wife, not
eating or sleeping.

Nefertari sat beside Merneptah's sleeping
pallet. She arranged the layers of her sheath.
"You are looking stronger today. There is rose
in your cheek." Merneptah's cheeks were so
colorless, they looked translucent, but Nefertari
wanted to cheer him. She smiled gently,
unaware of the physicians who were hypno-
tized by her graceful movements.

Merneptah coughed in spasms that wracked
his body. Nefertari pulled a scarf across her
face, staring at the pox oozing on Merneptah's
arms and chest. She wanted to reach out to
him, but she was afraid. She stroked her own
smooth skin, shuddering at the thought of the
pox spreading over her, eating her flesh. She
would have a slave massage balm into her skin

when she returned to her chamber. She pushed her chair back a bit.

"Is there some entertainment you wish? I could call forth the dancers."

Merneptah weakly shook his head. It was all he could manage.

It struck Nefertari that Merneptah might die. The thought of one of her own children on the throne flickered. She felt ashamed. Flustered, she rose to leave, then remembered her promise to Pharaoh and sat again.

"Mother," Merneptah whispered.

Nefertari turned. Istnofret was coming in.

The two wives nodded to each other; then Nefertari quickly left the sickroom in a cloud of fabric. Istnofret pulled a chair close to Merneptah's bedside, gathering him in her arms. "How are you feeling today, my son?"

"I am scared, Mother."

Istnofret stroked Merneptah's forehead. "What scares you?"

"What if I should die?"

She paused for just a second in her stroking to fight back her own tears. Her heart ached, but she spoke lightly. "To die is not a thing to fear. To drink from the waters of paradise on the journey to the afterlife is a gift from the gods. It is the natural order of things. Even Pharaoh must move on someday. Your ka will go first and prepare for your arrival."

"But what if the Devourer should find my sins too heavy?"

"You are the son of the Great God. The feather of truth will balance." Istnofret spoke with conviction, but then, even though she tried for Merneptah's sake to remain strong, a note of pleading crept into her voice. "But you must try to get well."

Merneptah lay back on his headrest. After his father's rage and Nefertari's fear, his mother's soft voice comforted him. Istnofret watched her son relax. She swallowed and began again.

"When you are Pharaoh, you will commission the Royal Architect to build a tomb that brings glory to your name. It will be filled with the toys of your youth and the tools of your manhood. There will be thousands of servants to see to your every need. It will be even more beautiful than the desert at sunset. Your place in the sun."

Istnofret spoke in a hushed voice, her words softening into silence. Merneptah had fallen asleep.

CHAPTER 9
The Governor of Nubia

The Governor turned the statue over in his hands. The gilded eyes of Sekhmet wept for him. He had a strange impulse to throw the statue against the wall. He shuddered. "You say a prisoner carved this?"

The guard stood at attention. "We caught him in the camp. Another prisoner betrayed him."

"Where is he now?" The Governor placed the statue in the center of his desk. The eyes followed him. It made him uneasy.

The guard stood straighter. "Being prepared for execution."

"Execution!" The Governor turned sharply to face the guard.

The guard was confused. "The rules are clear." His voice faltered and he drew back from the Governor's angry stare. "But sir, he stole gold from the mines."

"You fool, bring him to me at once." The Governor turned his back on the guard. "You had best pray for your unworthy ka that he still lives." The guard left the Governor's office running.

The Governor sat facing the statue. He was sick of the grit that permeated everything in this godless wasteland. His skin itched from the film that coated it. The dust mixed with his sweat to form a clay shell that cracked and crumbled whenever he moved. He closed his eyes and pictured the blue waters of the Nile. To be clean again . . .

He was no judge of great art; who would be, he thought, living in this colorless, barren outpost? But he knew from the prickling on the back of his neck that this was something powerful. Something rare.

Rumor had reached the mines that the Pharaoh's son lay ill at the palace, struck down by the plague. The Governor had heard that the Great One himself was desperate, willing to try anything for his son. It wouldn't hurt to bring this slave and his trinket north. If by some miracle it worked and cured the Pharaoh's son, the reward would be great. He'd get out of this stinking hole, maybe even have a choice of posts. Thebes—he'd stay in Thebes, perhaps even head the palace guard.

The Governor scratched his arm, his fingernails caked with grime. A hot bath every day. No choking on dust. The sound of shadufs creaking, their buckets swinging full of cool water from the Nile. The Governor licked his cracked lips.

A knock broke his daydream. "Enter."

The guard shoved the prisoner into the Governor's chamber. Off balance from weakness, the boy fell to his knees when the guard let go of his arm.

"What is your name?" They all looked alike, these vermin, flesh swinging loosely from their bones, eyes popping out of the filth that covered their faces. This one looked no different.

"Senmut, son of Yuf, master sculptor."

"You carved this?" The Governor thrust forward the statue of Sekhmet, holding it at arm's length.

Senmut looked at the statue gilded in the forbidden gold. His death certificate. He swallowed. "Yes, I carved the Great Healer."

The Governor studied the statue. He couldn't seem to stop looking at it. "Take him."

The guard grinned viciously. He took hold of Senmut's sidelock and yanked him to his feet.

"Gently, you fool."

The guard looked confused again. Gently? What did it matter? The criminal would be dead inside the hour.

The Governor never took his eyes off Sekhmet. "I want him cleaned up. Make him presentable. I'm taking him to the palace."

The guard stood still, sure that he could not have heard correctly. Senmut held his breath, not daring to believe his own ears. Was he dreaming?

The Governor scowled at the confused guard. "Move. Send word to prepare the barge. We leave for Thebes at first light."

CHAPTER 10
The Lion's Roar

Senmut clutched his statue to his chest. One guard marched in front of him and one behind. The Governor walked on ahead, his guards flanking him, pushing the citizens to the side.

The streets of Thebes were crowded and noisy; barkers traded their wares for bread and beer, servants fetched water from shadufs on the river's edge, and children ran between the legs of priests and tradesmen. Senmut laughed at a priest flailing his arms to keep from falling when a small boy knocked him off balance. The sound Senmut made was thin and cracked, and he realized it had been a long time since he'd laughed.

Senmut took a deep breath, savoring the smell of his city. It was good to be home. The guard stepped on his heel. "Keep up."

From somewhere in the crowd there came a lion's roar. Senmut smiled, remembering the time his friend Menkh had taught him to roar to keep the jackals at bay. It seemed a lifetime ago. Some shepherd must know his old friend's tricks.

The roar sounded again, closer. Senmut searched the crowd. The guard behind him grew impatient. "You'll lose the Governor. Hurry." Senmut sped up.

A boy shouldering an oversized papyrus basket fell in step alongside Senmut. "Care for a scarab, or perhaps an ant or two?"

"Menkh! I was sure you were dead!" Senmut wanted to hug his friend, but instead he looked around at the guard following him. The guard was watching the Governor.

"If not for some sand dwellers I would be. They peeled me off a sand dune. One criminal saving another." Menkh laughed.

"You are lucky they didn't slit your throat."

"They aren't so bad as that."

"It is good to see you, my friend. I hardly believe it. In all of Thebes, you!"

"I saw the Governor's standard flapping from his barge at the river's edge. Had to see what brought the jackal north. The last person I expected to see was you. How is it they bring you to Thebes?" Menkh asked, glancing around, on the lookout for trouble.

Senmut told Menkh of the statue and the Governor.

"So you have just landed, then?"

"Just."

"Well then, you don't know how blessed your statue truly is. I've been to see your family. Your father is alive and well—better, I would wager, when he hears of your fortune."

"He is well?" Senmut grabbed Menkh's arm.

"Amazingly."

The guard knocked the basket from Menkh's shoulder. "You. Out of the way."

Menkh scrambled to gather the spilled dates before they were ruined underfoot. The guard ground several into the dirt, grinning at

Menkh. Menkh spit on his foot. The guard grabbed hold of Menkh by both arms. Menkh struggled, but the guard held him firmly, lifting him off the ground. Menkh kicked the air.

"Stop." Senmut held the statue over his head. "I'll smash it, I swear by Amun. Let him go."

Irritated, the Governor turned around to see what was causing all the noise. He rushed back, waving his arms. "Let him go. I'll not risk my future over some filthy rag like this." The Governor's face was bright red.

The guard let Menkh loose. Menkh gave a swift bow to Senmut, then disappeared into the crowd.

"You are either very brave or very foolish," the Governor said, reaching for the statue.

"We'll never know, will we?" Senmut hugged the statue to himself.

"Oh, I think we shall know soon enough." The Governor flicked open a linen square and wiped his brow. "Everything depends on what happens to the Great One's son. If things go poorly with him, that trick could cost you your life."

Senmut should have been worried, he knew, but all he could think about was that his father was alive. He was well. And with Amun's will, Senmet might see his parents once again. From somewhere deep in the crowd came a lion's roar. Senmut lifted his head and roared back.

CHAPTER 11
A Place in the Sun

Merneptah's eyes fluttered open. The first thing he saw was an image. The image of the goddess Sekhmet. She hovered over his bed, suspended in air. She floated in a ball of light gathered and magnified from the sunlight that leaked through the shutters.

Merneptah reached for her. The movement brought him full awake. A statue of Sekhmet stood on a table at his bedside. He closed his eyes, pressed on his eyelids with his fingertips, then opened his them again slowly. Sekhmet remained solidly on the table.

Merneptah ran his tongue over his lips. His mouth was as dry as the desert. He raised himself on one elbow. His father overflowed the bedside chair, his upper body sprawled across the bottom of Merneptah's couch. He snored lightly.

Merneptah beckoned a servant with crooked finger and mouthed the word "Water." His father continued to snore undisturbed. The word had not left Merneptah's lips before a goblet appeared, sweating from the cold well water. Merneptah drank deep. He felt the coolness flow down his throat and disappear into his body. The second goblet he sipped at.

Peering over the brim, Merneptah looked around the room at physicians and priests, heads bowed in prayer. In the corner a ragged boy about his own age squatted, studying him intently. *He can't be a palace slave,* Merneptah thought. *He is all bones and rags. What is he doing here?*

Senmut felt uncomfortable under the sudden scrutiny of the Great One's son. He'd grown to know the sleeping face after watching it for two days now. Awake, the face looked different. Senmut was conscious of his torn clothing and bare feet. His body, once strong, was now little more than sticks wrapped in flesh. *He must think I'm a beggar.* Senmut straightened his back as best he could while still keeping his head below the level of the Pharaoh's.

Merneptah wondered what the boy was thinking. *The sickness has stolen my strength,* he thought. *It's left me pale and poxed. He must see me as weak, not fit to be the next Pharaoh. He must wonder how I will manage to make the waters of the Nile flood and the sun rise.*

Merneptah summoned a servant to put sandals on his feet. He sat on the edge of the couch. His head whirled. He tried to keep watching the boy, but the room darkened. When he was sure he was about to faint, the image of Sekhmet hovered in the darkness, glowing brighter, until slowly Merneptah's vision cleared. Sekhmet stood on the table. Merneptah reached out to touch her but stopped, his fingers extended, not more than a grain of sand's distance from her gilded face. And then he knew.

"You are the sculptor." It was not a question.

Senmut bowed his head.

Merneptah whispered, "She came for me in my sleep."

Senmut looked up at Merneptah, who struggled to hide the faint tremor in his weakened hand. *He is as shamed by his pitiful state as I am by mine,* Senmut thought. "It seems we have both known better times, times before Sekhmet's assistance was needed." Senmut looked down at his own wasted frame.

Merneptah smiled. "So you read thoughts as well."

"I need only look into my own heart." Senmut realized the boldness of comparing himself, a sculptor's son, to the son of a god. He flattened himself to the chamber floor.

"Father would not permit you in my chamber if he didn't find you worthy. Rise."

Senmut sat upright. "The Great God discovered that the statue healed my father when things looked hopeless. I think he prayed it would do the same for you. He loves you very much." Senmut had been surprised by Pharaoh's devotion to his son. It was so—so human, so mortal.

The voices nudged Pharaoh from his slumber.

He looked to the empty headrest, confused, not fully awake. Then, seeing his son sitting, his eyes widened and he lunged for Merneptah. He hugged him fiercely. "Praise Amun."

"And Sekhmet."

"And Sekhmet." The Pharaoh grabbed the statue and raised it over his head. "Praise Sekhmet." Ramses clapped his arm around his son's shoulder, crushing him to his side.

Merneptah reached for the statue, feeling warmth travel up his fingers when he touched the gilded goddess. "Her life force strengthens mine. I feel her heat."

"Our young sculptor has pleased the goddess with his art. She blesses us all. Call Neferronpet. Summon the scribes. Let it be known that Senmut, son of Yuf, is to be apprentice to the Royal Sculptor." Ramses smiled at Senmut. "That is, if it pleases him."

Everyone in the room turned to Senmut. He didn't trust his voice, so he just nodded.

Ramses smiled. "Then so be it."

Merneptah clasped the statue to his chest. "What is your name, sculptor?"

"Senmut."

"It is my wish that the name Senmut be heard always."

Senmut thought of the cavern of bodies at Nubia. Nameless corpses condemned to wander the Land of the Ghosts for eternity. His fate could have been the same but for the wood of an acacia.

Ramses II spoke. "When the day comes that Osiris calls Senmut to the afterlife, he shall have a place in the royal tomb where he can carve and watch over Merneptah for eternity. Senmut shall live forever. Senmut shall have his place in the sun."

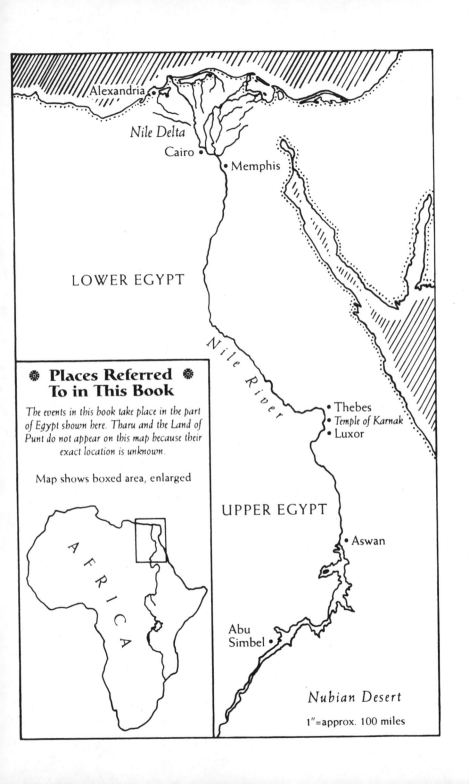

Alexandria •

Nile Delta

Cairo •

• Memphis

LOWER EGYPT

Nile River

A F R I C A

• Thebes
• *Temple of Karnak*
• Luxor

UPPER EGYPT

• Aswan

Abu
Simbel •

Nubian Desert

1″=approx. 100 miles

Abu Simbel (ah-boo SIM-bell)—southern site where Ramses II carved his Great Temple from the sandstone cliffs.

amulet (AM-yoo-let)—a small charm worn for protection or luck.

Amun (AH-mun)—the king of gods, thought to be the father of the pharaohs in the New Kingdom. Also spelled Amon or Amen.

ankh (onk)—the symbol of eternal life, a cross with a loop forming the top segment.

Anubis (uh-NOO-bis)—the jackal-headed god of embalming. The Egyptians believed that when someone died, Anubis weighed the person's heart against the feather of truth. If the deceased had been good during his earthly life, his heart would be light and would balance favorably with the feather of truth. Osiris, king of the dead, would then admit the deceased into the other world.

Bastet (BAHS-tet)—the cat goddess, daughter of the sun god, Re. She possessed the power to ripen the crops with the sun.

the Devourer—a monster, part lion, part crocodile, and part hippopotamus. If the heart of the dead, burdened by sin, tipped the scales against the feather of truth, the Devourer ate the heart. The Egyptians believed destroying the earthly body condemned the spirit, or ka, to wander the desert for eternity, never to enter the other world.

Eye of Horus (HAW-russ)—symbol believed to ensure good health.

Festival of Opet (OH-pet)—The most impor-
tant festival in Thebes, honoring Amun's
marriage. The golden statue of Amun, carried
by priests, left his temple at Karnak and jour-
neyed by barge to his temple in Luxor. At this
time commoners could request judgment from
Amun instead of a trial through the court sys-
tem. During the reign of Ramses II, the Festival
of Opet lasted twenty-four days.

Isis (EYE-sis)—goddess of protection.

Istnofret (IST-noh-fret)—Ramses II's second
chief queen. She was known for her intelli-
gence.

Ka (kah)—the life force, similar to a guardian
angel. When the body died, the ka entered the
underworld to prepare the way.

Temple of Karnak (CAR-nack)—the largest
sacred site in the world. Ramses II added a hall
to the structure during his reign. The hall had
122 columns that rose as high as 75 feet and
were covered with raised hieroglyphs depicting

Ramses II worshipping Amun. Each column was so big around, 100 men could stand on top.

Keeper of the Diadem—special custodian of the Pharaoh's crowns. Every job at the palace had a title: Washer of the Pharaoh, Chief Bleacher, Superintendent of the Clothes, Keeper of the Cloth.

Land of the Ghosts—the desert.

Land of Punt—foreign land from where the Egyptians imported incense and myrrh. The exact location is in question.

Luxor—modern Arabic name for southern Opet, an area in eastern Thebes.

Merneptah (mer-NEP-tah)—son of Ramses II and Queen Istnofret. He was fifty years old when he became Pharaoh.

Neferronpet (neh-fer-RON-pet)—Ramses II's administrator.

Nefertari (neh-fer-TAH-ree)—Ramses II's chief queen and favorite. She was known for her beauty.

New Kingdom—1550–1070 B.C. 18th–20th Dynasties. Ramses II ruled in the 19th Dynasty.

Nile—the river. *Egypt* means "the gift of the Nile." Egypt is barren and rocky with the exception of a long, narrow area running along the Nile. The river's rhythms divide the year into three seasons: the flood time, "time of inundation" (July–October); the planting time, "time of emergence" (November–February); and the "time of harvest" (March–June).

Nubia (NOO-bee-uh)—a region at Egypt's southern border. Nubia was known for its gold and copper mines.

Osiris (oh-SIGH-riss)—god of the under-world, who judged all people when they died.

papyrus (puh-PIE-russ)—versatile aquatic

reed plant used to make sandals, baskets, nets, even loincloths. Egyptians used the stalks to make boats, dried it for fuel, and ate the sprouts in salads. To make paper, they cut the long stems into strips, placed two layers at right angles, and pounded them flat with a mallet.

pharaoh—king of Egypt, thought to be a god.

Ramses II (RAM-seez)—ruler of Egypt during the thirteenth century B.C. His reign was marked with prodigious building. He fathered more than 150 children and ruled as pharaoh more than 60 years. Also spelled Ramesses.

Re (ray)—the sun god. Also spelled Ra.

Red Land—the desert.

sand dwellers—wild thieves who roamed the desert.

scribe—a person whose job was to write. Since the Egyptian language had over 700 hieroglyphs or symbols to learn, training began as early as nine years old and lasted five to ten years. A scribe's duties varied from those similar to an accountant's to writing personal letters.

Sekhmet (SEK-met)—the lion-headed goddess who caused and cured illness.

shaduf (shah-DOOF)—a device used to move water from the Nile into irrigation ditches. A boom is slung across an upright pole. A bucket hangs from one end of the boom; the opposite end bears a counterweight, which makes lifting a bucket full of water easy for one person. Shadufs are still used in Egypt today.

sidelock—children's heads were shaved except for a lock of hair on one side.

Tharu—a city deep in the desert, where criminals whose noses had been cut off as punishment for their crimes lived together.

Thebes—the capital of Egypt during the New Kingdom.

Thoth (thoth or toht)—ibis-headed god of wisdom.

the Two Lands—the two parts of Egypt formed by the Nile. Upper Egypt, to the south, is a long, narrow valley with strips of arable land along the river. In lower Egypt, to the north, the river spreads out over hundreds of miles, creating a delta of rich, lush, flat land. An Egyptian pharaoh wears the double crown, symbolizing his rule of the two lands, and is known as King of Upper and Lower Egypt. Also called the Two Kingdoms.